A New King

by Jenny Jinks and BlueBean

Lion looked out at his kingdom.

"I am too old to be king any longer,"

he said. "It is time someone else was king."

Everyone was sad. Lion was a great king,

but he had no children to give his crown to.

Who would be the next king?

"I know! We will have a competition,"
said Lion. "Whoever wins will be
the next king."

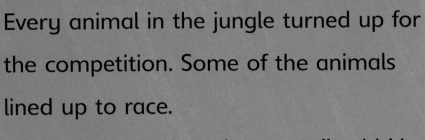

Every animal in the jungle turned up for the competition. Some of the animals lined up to race.

"I have set an obstacle course," said Lion. "You will need to be tough, brave and strong. Whoever finishes it will become the new king."

"On your marks.

Get set.

GO!"

Jaguar raced into the lead.

"This is easy. I will win for sure," she said.

But soon she reached the first obstacle.

A wide river crossed her path.

Jaguar hated water. She could not swim.

Turtle came along. He walked into the river and swam to the other side. Now he was in the lead.

"This is easy. I will win for sure," he said.

But then he came to the next obstacle.

A huge tree lay across the path. Turtle

could not go over it. Or under it. Or lift it.

Gorilla came along. He threw the tree into the air. It landed with a crash behind him, and he raced into the lead.

"This is easy. I will win for sure," Gorilla said.

But then he came to the next obstacle.

A huge tangle of thorn bushes blocked

the path.

Gorilla was much too big to get through.

The rest of the animals of the kingdom waited at the finish line.

They wanted to see who their new king would be. They watched and waited, but nobody came.

What if no animal could complete the obstacle course?

Then they heard a squeak.

"Down here," said Mouse as she crossed

the finish line. "I have won the race!"

All the animals looked at each other

in amazement.

"How can this be?" Lion asked.
"Surely a tiny mouse could never get
through my challenge on her own."
"I didn't," said Mouse.

"Aha! You cheated! I knew it! A mouse
could never be king," he laughed.

But Mouse went on. "I completed the challenge. I just didn't do it on my own," she said. "I knew Jaguar was fast, so I clung to her tail. I knew Turtle could swim, so I floated on his back. I knew Gorilla was strong, so I hopped on his shoulder. And when everyone got stuck in the thorn bushes, I was able to get through."

The animals looked at Lion.

Lion looked at Mouse.

Finally, Lion spoke. "Mouse knew all the animals. She knew how they could help her. That is a sign of a true king."

He took off his crown and gave it to Mouse.
Everyone cheered, "Hooray for
the new king!"

Story order

Look at these 5 pictures and captions.
Put the pictures in the right order
to retell the story.

1

Gorilla throws the tree.

2

Mouse is crowned king.

3

Jaguar races ahead at the start.

4

Mouse explains how she won the race.

5

Turtle cannot get over the big tree.

Independent Reading

This series is designed to provide an opportunity for your child to read on their own. These notes are written for you to help your child choose a book and to read it independently.

In school, your child's teacher will often be using reading books which have been banded to support the process of learning to read. Use the book band colour your child is reading in school to help you make a good choice. *A New King* is a good choice for children reading at Purple Band in their classroom to read independently.

The aim of independent reading is to read this book with ease, so that your child enjoys the story and relates it to their own experiences.

About the book

King Lion is tired of being king. He decides to hold a contest to see which animal is the best choice to replace him.

Before reading

Help your child to learn how to make good choices by asking:
"Why did you choose this book? Why do you think you will enjoy it?"
Look at the cover together and ask: "What do you think the story will be about?" Ask your child to think of what they already know about the story context. Then ask your child to read the title aloud. Ask:
"Why do you think there's going to be a new king?"
Remind your child that they can sound out the letters to make a word if they get stuck.
Decide together whether your child will read the story independently or read it aloud to you.

During reading

Remind your child of what they know and what they can do independently. If reading aloud, support your child if they hesitate or ask for help by telling the word. If reading to themselves, remind your child that they can come and ask for your help if stuck.

After reading

Support comprehension by asking your child to tell you about the story. Use the story order puzzle to encourage your child to retell the story in the right sequence, in their own words. The correct sequence can be found on the next page.

Help your child think about the messages in the book that go beyond the story and ask: "What kind of animal was expected to win the race? Why was Mouse able to win even though she is small?"
Give your child a chance to respond to the story: "What was your favourite part and why? Which animal did you think would win?"

Extending learning

Help your child think more about the inferences in the story by asking: "Do you think Mouse will make a good king? Why/Why not?"

In the classroom, your child's teacher may be teaching different kinds of sentences. There are many examples in this book that you could look at with your child, including statements, commands and questions. Find these together and point out how the end punctuation can help us decide what kind of sentence it is.

Franklin Watts
First published in Great Britain in 2020
by The Watts Publishing Group

Copyright © The Watts Publishing Group 2020
All rights reserved.

Series Editors: Jackie Hamley, Melanie Palmer and Grace Glendinning
Series Advisors: Dr Sue Bodman and Glen Franklin
Series Designers: Peter Scoulding and Cathryn Gilbert

A CIP catalogue record for this book is
available from the British Library.

ISBN 978 1 4451 7165 4 (hbk)
ISBN 978 1 4451 7166 1 (pbk)
ISBN 978 1 4451 7299 6 (library ebook)

Printed in China

Franklin Watts
An imprint of
Hachette Children's Group
Part of The Watts Publishing Group
Carmelite House
50 Victoria Embankment
London EC4Y 0DZ

An Hachette UK Company
www.hachette.co.uk

www.reading-champion.co.uk

Answer to Story order: 3, 5, 1, 4, 2